The Black Spot
&
Little Girl Blue

There are things in this world ,
Though you may not believe ,
That are not entirely,
What they seem to be .

Once, a long time ago...though on second thought,
perhaps not that long at all,
A girl called Blue,
walked her same walk home from school.

She was strange,
if you asked those who were, well, ordinary.
and what she wanted, more than anything,
was just to be like everyone else.
But what she was, was so much more.
A little girl filled with magic,
though not without a dose (or three!)
of melancholy.

Her eyes wondered over things that most would not.
Not straight ahead or in the places most know,
But up and down,
above her head and under her toes.

And her head filled with stories,
of where those things she saw may have been,
and where they may still go.

Suddenly, some way up the street,
upon a glance to her feet,
She saw the oddest thing.
Something she had not yet before seen.

A perfect Black Spot.

She stopped awhile and looked,
and as she moved left foot to leave,
the most peculiar thing happened!
That same Black Spot moved too.

With right foot,
slowly swung forward,
you wouldn't believe it!
(unless you were there too)
But the Black Spot moved with Blue...

She thought she may be imagining,
but carried on walking with the cloppity-clop of school shoes,
and following Blue,
came the cloppity-clop of that same Black Spot.

She ran, then slowed, then skipped, then froze,
And all she did,
the Black Spot did too.
She giggled and smiled,
and let out at a "WOOOHOOOO!"

And she thought many different things.
"Maybe it's ink spilled from the writings of a conjurer's spell,
or a stolen magic ring which from a crow's beak fell.
A secret whispered and sworn not to tell,
or a coin tossed eons ago in some forgotten well".

As she reached home,
backpack into a bedroom corner thrown,
she lay on her bed,
and found that the Black Spot followed her,
to the pillow where she lay her head.

"I know what you are!
The pupil from an Empress's eye!
When stricken with grief over a love lost,
fell with her tears to the ground!", Blue cried.

"Whatever you are, my name is Blue,
And I think I'll call you....Dot", the girl said with glee.
And Dot seemed to agree.
And so it was for a while, Blue and Dot.
A girl once lonely, now never felt alone.

Most nights, lying tangled in her coal-dark hair,
Dot would listen and look,
as Blue shared her dreams and read her favourite books.
For finally she had a true friend.
And the closer they became,
the less Blue cared about all the other things "out there".

The Scarlet

And soon Dot would speak,
close to ear,
growing ever so big.
Looking less like a spot,
but something darker still.
With lips that would part,
and limbs that could bend,
whispering words,
sworn as secrets between these two friends..

"Oh, I'd never tell Dot! It's just you and me,
Just like you say. No-one else matters,
Just me and you", Blue would say reassuringly.
But the bigger it grew,
the more Blue felt small.

The cloppity-clop of school shoes,
walking home from school,
soon became the dragging of feet,
And the loneliness Blue thought had gone,
felt somehow lonelier now,
as she wondered...inside her head
"Who is Dot? And who is Blue?
I can no longer tell who is who".

And so it cast shadows over everything.
And the girl that looked up and down,
and all around,
felt that her magic,
that special something which made her different from the rest,
was now stolen, not given.

Wondering maybe,
if that friend found on the street,
was really no friend at all,
but a thief.

And so Blue now small and Dot big,
the girl that gave everything to not be lonely,
and wished to be simply ordinary,
invited something darker in.

Remember when I said:

"There are things in this world,
Though you may not believe,
That are not entirely,
What they seem to be?".

Well, think of that Black Spot,
and if you find yourself in doubt,
thinking it can't be true,
think instead of that little girl called Blue.

And instead of trying to be ordinary,
cherish that magic within which makes you,
well...YOU!